Martian Love Tomes

By Michael G. Jones

ISBN: 0-7596-4111-0

This book is printed on acid free paper.

1stBooks - rev. 4/3/02

INTRO WITH ANECDOTE

By Michael G. Jones 5/15/92

Threadbare Sanity,

Is certainly no mere way of life, nor description thereof.

It is, afterall,

Light,

And, loose; no longer being bound by the material.

I pick my mind from its' pocket,

Mindlessly allowing it to drift, wherever.

Floating gently, upon arrival, thereof,

It appears to just be laying there,

Amidst the dust, thereof.

No one even notices.

All simply ignore.

It is swept away along with all the rest;

The dust,

The debris,

The camoflage of the warrior.

No one will even care,

Or, ever even know it is me,

On a journey past forever.

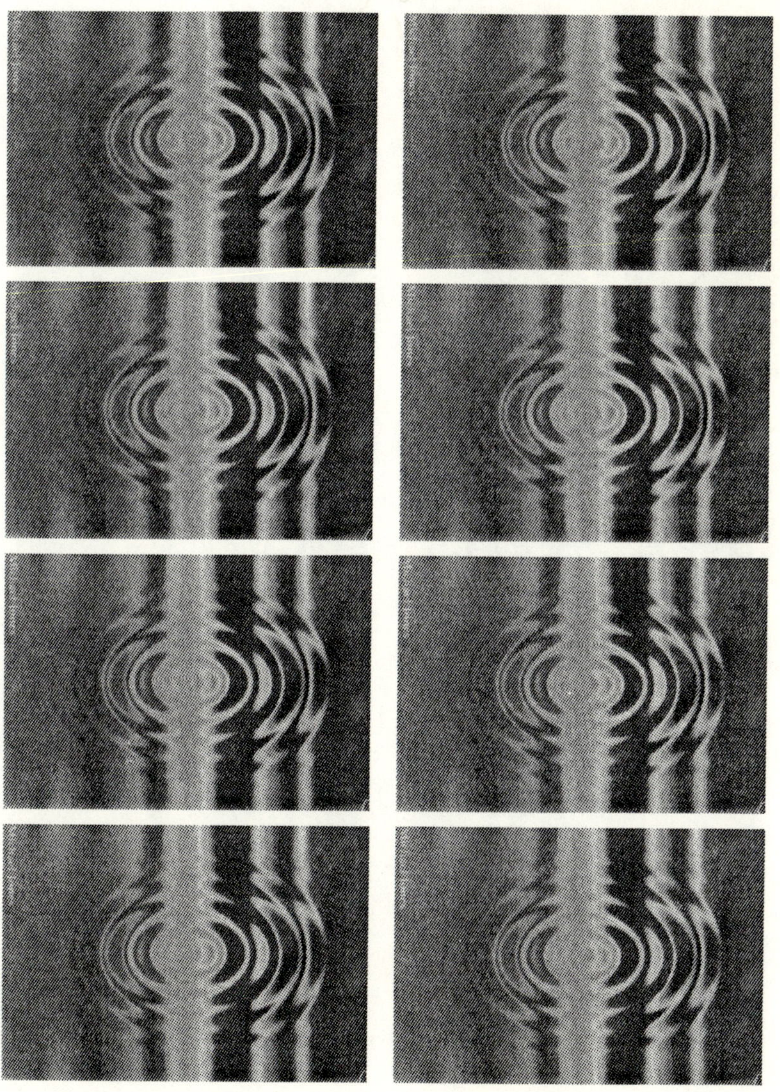

Just Standin' There

by Michael G. Jones

Just standin' there on the corner.
Just another fool on the wrong block.

Just standin' there on the corner.
Just another fool on the wrong block;
and the rain continued to pour.

I knew I had to give you somethin'
Somethin you never had before.

I knew I had to give you somethin'
Somethin' ... that you really did need.

I knew I had to give you my Good Love,

Because my Good Love,

Could set you free.

You were lookin', oh so lonely.

Oh so, pretty.

Oh so, sad.

I knew I had to give you my Good Love;

The Best,

And the Best,

you ever had.

The kind of Love you never had before.

The kind of Love that can open any door;

So, just when you thought you had had enough of Love,

My Good Love could give you so much more......,

Oh so much more.

Michael G. Jones

My Good Love's a kind love,

Though some say it's a Blind Love.

My Good Love's the kind that you find,

That you simply can't,

Ignore.

I could just dismiss that vault you reside in.

The one you hide in your heart in;

Just dismiss that veil of sorrow,

Before you say tomorrow;

But, I could never beg, steal, or borrow,

To give you this Good Love I've got.

And while I was just standin' there;

Standin' so unaware,

I knew I had to give you somethin'.

I knew I had to give my Good Love to show you,

How much that I care.

How much I,

Really do care

That when your hand touched my hand,
My heart had already been taken,
Then your eyes whispered;
"Take my Good Love,.....Take it,...
Take it, if you dare."

Was it just my imagination?
Or something in the air?
But, I knew I had to give you my Good Love,
And Good Love,
Was all I had to share;
All I had to share.

And a good five minutes had passed by,
Before I fell for you.
Okay, so, maybe I'm not telling the truth.
Okay, so, maybe it was only, more like two.

Michael G. Jones

Love at first sight,

On an ordinary night,

On an ordinary, rainy night,

While simply,

Just standin' there.

It Takes Time

by

Michael G. Jones

It was the best of times,

It was the worst of times,

It was one of the worst crimes of all times.

And what really blows my mind,

Is that there was no sign,

No fault or blame I could hold onto.

No roaring sound of thunder;

Only the sorrow of the crash.

It really tore my world asunder.

It came on me just like a flash.

But, it ain't no permanent solution.
No. it don't fit my priorities at all,
When I wake up in the night,
And I know everything's alright.
It's just that I still keep hopin' you'll call.

And I tell myself this is the last time.
This is the last time I'll dream of you;
Because that phone never rings,
And it's just one of those things.
It's just one of those things that's true.

Did it have to be such a good thing?
Did it have to be the best time of all?
Did it have to be love that tore us apart?
Could you really call that Love, at all?

I'm not talkin' about no Revolution; no Revelation;
Just the end of time.
Because I'm talkin' about the Love that died, girl;
The Love between me and you.

And I've been thinkin' about the Good Times,
Though sometimes they do seem far and few;
And though I hurt deep inside,
And it's a hurt I can't hide,
Somehow the Good times do seem to pull me through.

Sometimes I still get lonely,
Yeah girl, I still get lonely for you;
And just one thing sets me free;
And it's your memory.
It's all that's left, so,
It has to do.

With just a song in the night,

To hold me tight;

To try and hold out for just one more day.

Anyway,

Most of all, Girl, I still really love you.

Most of all, Girl, I do still love you.

Yes, I still really do;

Really do Love You,

..........Most of All.

LOVE is: Tres Camus & Quai Chang, too: (True or False)?

by Michael G. Jones

Love is lonesome and cold as can be:

Waiting for the fire that you set inside of me;

Waiting for your fire to come and burn me up;

Waiting for your fire to come and set me free.

Love is like when I'm alone waiting just for you.

Love is pearl handeled, cobalt and blue.

My heart is your target and your aim is true.

Love is like a Stranger.

Michael G. Jones

One thing about Love I should make perfectly clear,

Is Darlin', from my Love, you know, you should have no fear,

Because,

Love is like the one that gets you;

Love is like the one you never hear.

Darlin' my Love won't ever leave you in any danger.

Because,

My Love, you know,

My Love is like a Stanger.

Darlin' another thing about Love even stranger still,

Is, Love, my Love, you know, is kind of just like a thrill,

Except when Love is ill;

When Love is misbegotten.

Then Love is surely nothing that is fancy.

Though you know how I love the audience in the Paris video sequence,

In the Movie, "Sid & Nacy".

Love is like Life: a Movie, a Beach.
Love is like a Prisoner: out touch; out of reach.

Oh yes, and of course, Love is also to Teach.
I don't want to seem like one to have to want to Preach,
But, Darlin' you know, Love is whatever Love is,
Whatever Love is to each.

Whatever Love is, Love seems to always take two.
I've added it all up, and the sum total of Love equals you.
Your Heart is my target and my aim will be true.

Love is like a Stanger.

WE GO ON

There we were,
Myself and her,
Finding each other, at last.

Now we go on.
Somewhere we went wrong.
Our love's just a thing in the past,

And, the solitary corporealness.
That combines, communicates,
And, is agreed on,
To become the Future,
Prematurely,
Comes and grows,
Much too fast.

by
Michael G. Jones

4/26/99

Naturally

by

Michael G. Jones

By the Grace of the one above,
It's time to show each other, all about Love.
It's the kind of thing, (Yeah, I'm talkin' 'bout Love!!),
We're just not ever going to get enough of.

From the first time I saw you,
There was nothing I could do.
I could feel it through and through.
Our love would be as strong as it is true.

Baby, we're going to take it all the way.

To forever, day by day;

With love's help, I hope and pray.

Crazy, in love we're going to stay.

All just part of Love's lovin' plan,

(Guy) "You'll be my lovin' woman."

(Gal) "I'll be your lovin' woman."

(Guy) "And, I'll be your lovin' man.

(Gal) "You'll be my lovin' man."

Straight up, now, darlin',

Please say you understand.

We'll always stay together,

Just as close as we ever can.

And, we'll finally surrender,

Just like we began,

To a love, so tender,

Time and time,

And time, again.

7/7/1999

ENDLESSLY

by Michael G. Jones

Your love song,

Lulls me into reverie,

With its loving charm,

Its passion, and its melody;

Where I Rap, Rap, Rapturously repose,

And I suppose,

I'm all about you,

Endlessly.

That's just the way it goes.

Not only heaven knows.

And, as our love song grows,

Like fields of chordal harmonies,

We'll take love's to's and fro's;

Take the highs and lows.

We'll change them to Rap Rhapsodies.

Now, not only Heaven knows,

That,

That's just the way it goes,

Because I love you,

I suppose.

If something goes wrong,

Or, if I feel blue,

I just close my eyes, and,

Picture you.

A more pleasant vision,

I could never see.

A more sincere affection,

There could ever be.

Yes love,

Your love songs,

Caress me into ecstasy,

With their loving charm,

Their passion, and their melody.

Your love is the love I chose,

So, not only Heaven knows,

That,

That's just the way it goes.

And, when the music is finally thru,

With songs of me and you,

We'll still have eternity.

That's just the way it's meant to be;

On and on, together,

Endlessly.

Not only Heaven knows,

I suppose,

Because you love me.

2/1/93

"Yeah, But...."

by

Michael G. Jones

Why when you all talk about us women,
You call us Bitches, or Hoochies, or Ho's?

Well, it's just the upper hand Dudes have tried to keep up,
Since the Beginning;
A sure sign of insecurity,
And it shows.

Yeah, but....
Why when you all talk about us women,...
You call us Bitches, or Hoochies, or Ho's?

Michael G. Jones

You see, we keep teaching our fears,

To drown in our beers.

It goes on and on,

It's the same with our tears.

Putting on the Man Mask.

It's a task I can play off to my Homeys.

The Man in the Mirror still knows.

Yeah, but....

Why when you all talk about us women,

You call us Bitches, or Hoochies, or Ho's?

Well, it's Just that you Ladies pride and concern yourselves,

About being the sex objects of our affection and perplexion,

When really,

You're just merely,

The dear objects of our woes.

Yeah, but....

Why when you all talk about us women,

You call us Bitches, or Hoochies, or Ho's?!!!

You see, it's the real life communications,

Of the most meaningful Human Relations, and,

Further evidence of HOW A TRULY PROGRESSIVEE, DECADENT

'SOCIETY', grows.

Yeah, but,.....

You know,

..................like,

When you all talk about us women?

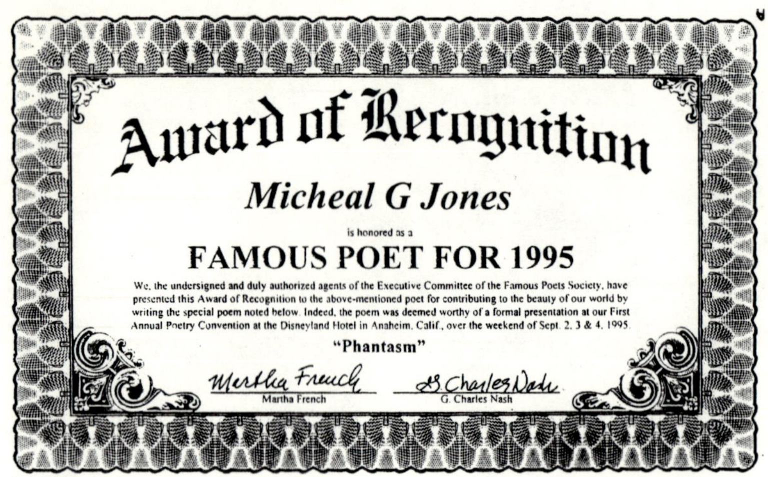

Award of Recognition

Micheal G Jones

is honored as a

FAMOUS POET FOR 1995

We, the undersigned and duly authorized agents of the Executive Committee of the Famous Poets Society, have presented this Award of Recognition to the above-mentioned poet for contributing to the beauty of our world by writing the special poem noted below. Indeed, the poem was deemed worthy of a formal presentation at our First Annual Poetry Convention at the Disneyland Hotel in Anaheim, Calif., over the weekend of Sept. 2, 3 & 4, 1995.

"Phantasm"

Martha French — G. Charles Nash

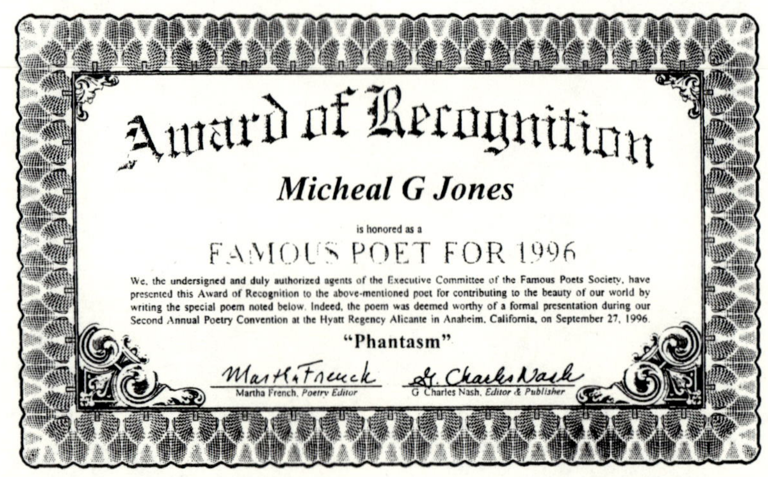

Award of Recognition

Micheal G Jones

is honored as a

FAMOUS POET FOR 1996

We, the undersigned and duly authorized agents of the Executive Committee of the Famous Poets Society, have presented this Award of Recognition to the above-mentioned poet for contributing to the beauty of our world by writing the special poem noted below. Indeed, the poem was deemed worthy of a formal presentation during our Second Annual Poetry Convention at the Hyatt Regency Alicante in Anaheim, California, on September 27, 1996.

"Phantasm"

Martha French, *Poetry Editor* — G. Charles Nash, *Editor & Publisher*

A pre-Consecration of Relationship Agreement

(unbinding) pending and somewhat tentative, if not approved.

CLAUSE A:

1. The Party of the First Sex and the Masculine Person both agree that the formality of such a Document can both enhance the enjoyment, and Increase the benefit of any intended present and Future understandings, or, possible intimacies
2. This sort of document should only be considered or assigned to relationships ranging in emotional intensity, from casual to mildly intense, and does not adequately detail any of a more extreme nature.

   SUBSECTION a.) In the realm of extreme nature may be Included progeny, i.e., children or pets.

CLAUSE B:

1. Neither Gender shall exploit emtionally, spiritually, economically, nor physically, one's complimentary gender.

SUBSECTION a) In the Realm of physical may be Included, abuse.

SUBSECTION b) This is also the case for The Realm of "emotional" and "economical."

Therefore, not indicated is licence

Or permission to extort or steal from

Each other, including kisses, hearts,

Bodily fluids, property, or possessions.

SUBSECTION c) Also included in all three Realms is the Intent of this document, and the Trust That this is the only agreed upon Document of its type on behalf of both Parties signed, reflecting the Mutually exclusive and loving quality.

2. Both parties agree that each will employ at all times, safe sex to the fullest extent that it is comfortably possible without endangering lives.

CLAUSE C:

1. This agreement can be mutually reviewed, amended, or updated at any time or place.
2. This agreement can be mutually ignored, thereby terminated with consequence at any agreed upon place and time, for the term of any agreed upon duration.
3. This is the case for either the entirety, or any agreed upon portion or quality of the relationship.

IF FELT NECESSARY, THIS DOCUMENT MAY BE APPROVED BY A PUBLIC NOTARY

DATE:

NECESSARY..______.....UNECESSARY..______.

SIGNATURES:1.____________________________

2.____________________________

THE SOLITUDE OF TWO

ONE

by Michael G. Jones

Me,

Apart from You;

Even if you're only just over a Hugs length

away.

The distance is Intolerable;

An Eternity of indeterminable Obtuse.

Objections, Obstructions?

Overtime!

Word OUt.

The Un-Trap

By Michael G. Jones

He caught himself;

Behid eyes wanting to gleam;

Laughlingly knowing things aren't always as they seem;

And the nightmare ended,

With a silent last desparate scream,

As they awoke,

Together,

Dreaming the dream.

She caught him.

While he tried to remove her mote,

She craftily helped remove his beam,

So that,

They could no more hide from love.

So that,

In love,

Together,

They made ever always,

An unvanquishable team.

DARK ART JURISPRUDENCE

By Michael G. Jones

In all the fairly quiet durations of emptiness,

That partition,

The currents,

Conveying,

The picture

That describes what becomes our life,

I find,

More often than not,

Not one,

Elysian

Illusion

Incidence

Or,

Occurence,

Where,   I don't think of you.

Finding instead,

That,

Life,

And that,

That   Sustains

The Gift,

Are   All   Inseparable

Even

By,

Distance,   Death,   Or, Time.

One curious reminder, though,

That is,

I mean,

I find   That Intimacy lets

The Worlds'   Poetry

Grow   More   Kind,

So, some of it's lines still rhyme,

............The colors of this Particular Painting.

I AM

By Michael G. Jones

Still,

Dwelling,

On the precipice;

Still,

Standing,

On the premise,

That we are all basically,

Good.

Not given to the grandiosity and vanity of

Miracles,

Much,

Any longer,

I only did,

What,

I could.

WRITE ON!

By Michael G. Jones

The Moving Finger
The Tell-Tale Heart
The Righteous Rocker's
Performance Art!

Where Desire leads
All Those who care.
Where Angels fear.
Where Eagles Dare!

Up From The Skies

By Michael G. Jones

Jimi Hendrix cried to be heard.
Very few understood a single word.
He wrote, "Spanish Castle Magic",
And his death as so tragic.

In, "Freedom", he told about the Drugstore Man.
You know his death was part of the Man's plan,
But,
Who did they/we kill, "Easy Rider", or, "Astro Man"?

He told us, "Castles Made of Sand" fall,
To the sea, eventually,
And that not only those with "Gypsie Eyes",
Would come to see,
That in "1983, A Myrrman I Should Be",

One day we will meet across the "Rainbow Ridge".
"Dolly Dagger" will step right out of her fridge.
"Angel" will come down without having to make,
another "Crash Landing".
Then, "Midnight Lighting" won't find it so demanding,
That, together we can't be destructed by that,
Apparent "Pali Gap";

To fullfil J's "One Rainy Wish" that,
As our ancestors clap.
His "Message to Love" won't go unrequited,
And "With The Power of Soul",
The "Voodoo Chile's" smile will be ignited.

"All Along The Watchtower" we'll be "Driftin'".

Where we won't even have to just ask,

The "Axis, Bold As Love",

When and If-Then,

The "Promised Land"'s time will have already begun,

And the People will see it, like a "New Rising Sun".

NIGHT BLIND

By Michael G. Jones

All things are contained by,

The Night;

All things,

Including the Light;

All her visible colors, and what remains in her absence,

Which is so degradingly called,

Not even a color.

All dreams, schemes, and themes,

Are touched by the Night's embrace;

All creatures, great and small;

Although, not even the wisest owl of keenest sight,

Has seen the true nature of the Night,

Nor,

Discerned the totality of the Night's face.

Not even being a color,

Some might be led to believe,

The Night,

Nonexistent and beyond belief.

In my love's absence,

I see nothing else.

In my love's absence.

I am,

Made painfully aware of,

The Night's existence,

At each and every infinetly slowly passing

moment's

Insistence.

LABYRINTH OR LOVE

By Michael G. Jones

In my hidden lairs,
Safe from strangers stares
You know I live life on the run.

The more I tried to hide,
The louder my soul cried,
Because it knew you were the one.

Even through my maze of craze,
Your love knew my true ways.
I guess I always knew you'd find me.

You caused my barriers to melt.
You knew everything I felt.
Now, my madness only crawls behind me.

Your love is such a thrill,
It left my horrific indulgence standing still.
It would be insane to think of keeping up
Because it knows it never will.

It is nearly undone.
Love has nearly won.
This is only because,
Our Love has only just begun.

100% WOMAN

by MICHAEL g. JONES

An abundance of,
Astral,
Anguish,
Attacks me,
With, Furious,
Fists of,
Frustrations.

The Silents Screams of Quiet
Desparation become,
Echos,
Reflected all over my Face.

My Body becomes a drooling mass of
expectation;
A confusing conflicting contrast;
A complex of sensation.

My Soul's perplexed,
Alone and lost,
It seems Somewhere,
Out in Space.

Over you,
100% Woman,
Nothing more and nothing less.
Yes, you're 100%,
100% Woman,
And Woman, you're the Best!

Next, your Body disrupts my Hope for concentration,
And your sex has put me in my place,
As I anxiously await your next voluptuous,
Demonstration,
Of just how justified your Integrity is,

As it strands me here in this Sphere of fear,
And the depths of despair and disgrace;
I pray you'll always stay,
My 100% Woman,
Because <u>your</u> Love's the One I can't replace.

Because you're not here beside me,
I tearlessly cry my self to sleep,
With a Spirit so torn apart by torment,
That only God would want to try and keep.

And, I dream a dream of dreaming,
Of dreaming a dream of dreaming a dream,
Of dreaming a dream of dreaming a dream,
Of dreaming, of dreaming a dream of dreaming a,
Dream,

Where my guitar has no need to weep or moan,
And, I'll be 100% TRUTHFUL,
100% Woman,
When I dream,
I am not alone.

Because you're 100%,
100% Woman,
A dream come true, I must confess.
Yes, you're 100%
100% Woman.
Because of you,
I Am,
Truly Blessed.

THE HEART OF THE MATTER

By Michael G. Jones

The door neither opens nor closes,
A lady sits on the edge of the chair,
In front of the mirror and dimly poses.

I can't guess what sights there she sees,
I, myself can hardly bear the suspense,
Of suspense filled moments such as these.

I, myself can only see the humor.
Coming from the horror,
Coming from the six o'clock T.V. News.

Yet, even Teenage Mutant Ninja Turtles,
Help to counter the Blues,
Emanating from my sometimes more than short,
Tempered, more than psychic fuse.

So, since we spent over thirty dollars,
You'd think we'd have been able to buy,
Her some, well, a little more,
Ladylike shoes,
And although it seems we aren't winning,
I know we just can't lose.

I don't even have to answer,
The phone that can't afford to be there, as,
She reclines, reposedly, further back,
In the more than well worn chair.

The lady becomes,
More and more my reason,
Why I still continue to care.

While we continue to patiently wait here,
Not knowing why, completely.
Perhaps, paying some dues of a Nature,
Mystic, Token.

As, in many ways,
The Destroyer of Death,
Remaining forever open, solitary,
With soliloquies of serenity,
Remaining forever,
Unspoken;
Freely available for any to use,
The Door neither closes nor opens;
. . . . . .Any Which Way We Choose.

"THE EARTH? THAT'S GOOD!"

by Michael G. Jones

I thought the daylight,
Out,
Up,
Over the Horizon.
I was slightly dismayed.
I hadn't expected the night to run and hide like
That.
I thought that for each other they were made.
I was played! They were just evening shade and
fade.

Sometimes,
I'm thinking I might just erase the scared little
Perverts.

"What should I use to separate,
the Firmament,
from the,
Heavenly Firmament,"
I also wondered?

"What a Mass!"
"This place really stinks!"
"Put it out on the furthest rim of the Galaxy!"
"What it really needs is a Good Bath!"

UNKNOWN ROCK STARS

@?2/10/91

By Michael G. Jones

You can say what you want,
You can say what you please,
But, this ain't another song about a nuclear freeze;
Because we're the unknown Rock Stars from a
forgotten time,
In another unpleasant, unpopular war....overseas:
Locking onto the steps of the Steppes;
Daydreaming about our fortune and fame;
Our women, our men, our guitars,
And, our Reps.
Locking onto our youthful ways;
Locking onto our innocent ways.
These are the days;
The Good ones.

Are we just another passing phase,
Working that Rock and Roll craze,
Struggling past our own youthful Rage,
Now less than half our present age.
Are we just another page.
Don't want to be just another page.
Ain't gonna be just another page;
Not another rotten page.

Gonna send our Platoon Leader to see the Samurai
Shrink,
Because we love this world even if she does stink.
Our leader best think twice,
Because this world. She's pretty nice.
Think I'll send my Shrink, too.
Yeah, that's that I'm gonna do.

You got to change your ways, baby,
Before the Samurai Shrink starts locking onto you.

3/10/98

J.C.&mE

By Michael g. Jones

You really changed the way I thought
I thought.
You really changed the way I feel.

You really changed the way I see all
The things I do.
You really changed it, now,
Only you can make it really real.

You really changed my blues right
Into bliss.
You really changed my life with just
One kiss.
You really changed what it was that
Was supposed to be our deal.

You really changed a one time
Chance happening.
You really changed it to a forever
Thing.
Now, I can take whatever changes
Time may bring,
Because you really changed into my
Everything.
You even changed this nowhere
Song I sing.
You're my one and only,
Changeling.
I really love you, so much, my Little
Ms. Changething.
My Darling Changeling, here's
Something that is really strange.
This is one thing you'll never
Changeling change.
Yes, there's one change you'll never

Put me through!

You'll never change me from into

Loving you!

IT WAS A BREEZE

By Michael G. Jones

10/31/9 D.

Carrying the Tumultous Turns,
That do be the Light,
That becomes divinely firmament,
She not only rocks steady across the surface of the Deep,
She knocks him to his Everlovin' knees.

"It's just the wind,"
He Cries,
Between the Heavenly sighs,
Beyond her Forbidden Zone;
Though,
If I'm not mistaken,
It's both of them who moan.

"Enough of your lies!"

She Screams,

Mere mortals are apparently deaf,

The very powers of Creation are shaken;

Giving rise to the Seas of Love,

Of which,

There be Seven.

"Reality,"

She Whispers,

"It's all completely overblown,"

"It's just the wind,"

He more gently Cries,

Between those same raptuous.........., sighs,

By the look in her eyes though,

If I'm not mistaken,

Her Heart is Overthrown.

"I guess he's just still too Bad to the Bone,"

She flatly Grumbles,

Yeah,....Right!

But, Bet!...

She still Comes,......

Otherwise, <u>you</u> explain,

Just how and why we all come to be here!

"It's just the wind,"

He Cries,

"It's just the wind."

But, the whole world knows he's just full of it.

A.B.T.

By Michael G. Jones

She's my Bigtime Angel.
I call her Angel Bigtime.
Because she's my Bigtime Angel,
And she's my angel Bigtime.

Everytime I see the girl,
She is in a different world,
But, inside her is a Pearl,
Bigtime.

She's my Bigtime Angel.
She's my Angel Bigtime.
I even call her angel Bigtime,
Because she's my Angel Bigtime.

Bigtime Angel, Angel Bigtime,
Has her Bigtime Angel dreams,
And Bigtime Angel angles,
For all her Angel Bigtime schemes,
Which we spend our time debatin',
And Bigtime Angel contemplatin'.

You see, Bigtime Angel, Angel Bigtime,
Likes to sometimes fuss and fight.
Sometines my Angel Bigtime never even treats me right.
But, I love my angel Bigtime.
She's Bigtime Angel delight.
Yeah, she's my Angel Bigtime.
She's such a Heavenly sight.

She's my Bigtime Angel.
I call her Angel Bigtime.
She's my Bigtime Angel,
And, she's my Angel Bigtime.

Michael G. Jones

I love my Angel Bigtime.
She's Bigtime Angel nice,
Never makes me frown.
You know she takes me to Paradise,
Bigtime Angel twice,
Everytime she loves me down.
Heaven sure must be missing my Angel Bigtime;
The Bigtime Angel that I found.

Anytime I see the girl,
She can really rock my world,
But, inside her is a Pearl,
Bigtime.

Yeah, she's my Bigtime Angel.
She's my Angel Bigtime.
I even call her Angel Bigtime,
Because she's my Angel Bigtime.

DREAMSTALKER

By MichaEL G. Jones

THE WIND AND,
STREETLIGHT,
TOOK ME ON A NIGHTFLIGHT,
SEARCHING
EVERYWHERE IN SIGHT
FOR MY
DREAMLOVER DELIGHT.
I CRASHED HARD
UPON,
UPON COMING ACROSS HER WALL
OF SOUL.
I LOST CONTROL ~
BUT, i RELISHED

THE ROLE........BECAUSE I DON'T

JUST TALK,

............OKAY, MAYBE i DO

DREAMSTALK HER,

A LITTLE,

AND, YOU KNOW, I REALLY LOVE

TO ROCK AND ROLL,

MY LITTLE RAMBLER

FOR YOU

By MichaEL g. jONES

Being a person,
Beginning,
To know Love,
Might not be able to see,
Immediately,
The divine completeness of yourself.

It is, however,
Essential,
That you must know
That
You are,

Seaven manifested,

In absolute beautific,

Female womb/manly, womanness flesh,

Inspires, and makes perfect,

throughly, by what is apparently from above,

and, obviously from within.

Now, know this,

A N G E L:

If you could only,

See

All that you truly

Are to

Me,

Respondantly, Rapslendantly,

You would Radiate Reminiscently in a

Rap, Rap, Rapturous Repose,

And, Remebering,

Me, in times of,

Reverie,

Grin or maybe giggle at Mr. Ridiculous,

Or, at least,

Sigh and smile,........I suppose.

Perhaps,

Maybe, only Heaven knows.

THE DELICATE DELECTABLE

BY SKYWALKER 12/16/1996

THERE, THERE,

THE MASSAGING FILAMENTS OF DISTANT
HYDROGEN FUSION,
GIVE LIFE TO THE ILLUSION;
PERMEATE AND UNCOVER THE SHAPES, FORMS,
AND, MAYBE EVEN THE FANTASIES,
OF LANDSCAPE AND HER INHABITANTA.

AND, QUITE THE FANTASIES THEY ARE, AT
THAT.
THEY'RE BOREDOM FOR SOME,.....
REGULATORY FISCAL AMBIGUITY FOR OTHERS.

MY FOCUS OF DEVOTION, HOWEVER,

NOTICES ONLY THE QUAINT FOREST,

AND THE SINFUL, SUPERFICIAL SKYLINE IT

OBVISCATES.

HER MOOD NOW GORGEOUSLY OBLITERATED,

SHE NUDELY CONTEMPLATES,

FIRST, A VOLUPTUOUS WINGED VICTORY,

SOARING ABOVE A SOON TO BE VINDICATED,

RESPONSE,

TO SUCH ATMOSPHERE,

AND, ITS' HABITATS OF MOCK OCCUPANTS,

SUBSTANTIALY SENTIENT AND CORPOREAL;

SECONDLY,

TEA AND EXERCISE,

(SPECIFICLY, ORGASM, IF SENSORY

ACKNOWLEDGEMENT OF THE

DANCE OF ETERNITY CAN EVER BE LESS THAN

EXISTENTIAL).

BESIDES,......

SHE WAS SHAKIN'!!!

I MEAN THROUGHLY PUT TOGETHER!

TO,.....

THAT IS,

FOR A NAKED SINGULARITY, THAT IS.

AND, WHAT'S YOUR MIDDLE NAME"?

by Skywalker *12/15/199*
6 circa A.D.

I DON'T REMEMBER MUCH ABOUT YOUR HANDS'
YET.

I DON'T REMEMBER MUCH DETAIL ABOUT WHAT
YOUR HANDS APPEAR TO REALLY LOOK
LIKE IS WHAT I ACTUALLY MEAN.

YET, FAR FROM FORGETTABLE,
THEY ARE LIKE YOUR EYES,
IN WAYS,
AND, SOME OF WHA T THEY'VE SEEN

LIKE THE YOU,
I, MYSELF,
AND ALL WITH THE GOOD FURTUNE,

TO BE ABLE TO,
BEHOLD,
THEY ARE BEAUTY AND LOVING INCARNATE,
SO,

I AM REMINDED MOMENTARILY AND EXPLICITLY
OF PRECISELY
HOW GLORIOUS THEY FEEL.

WITH TENDERNESS AND GENTLE CARING,
THEY BRUSH AND STROKE FALSE CLARITY TO ABSTRACTION,
AND, REPLACE IT WITH WHAT IS REAL.

ON THE ONE HAND,
THEY HAVE A GREAT AND TERRIFYING EXPLOSIVE POWER,
THAT CAN SHATTER BODY, MIND, AND SOUL.

ON THE OTHER HAND,

THEY HAPPILY COMFORT,

WITH EXQUISITE PLEASURE; COMMUNICATE

AND HEAL.

WITH DELIGHT I ENVISION THE FINGERTIPS

OF YOUR HANDS,

CARRESSING YOUR PERFECT LIPS,

. . . . .AND, OTHER PLACES,

THAT RHYME;

STILL,

. . . . .OTHERS OF A PARALLEL, BUT NOT

OF A PERFECTLY DISSIMILAR NATURE,

IF NOT OBSCURE AND DIVERSE IN FUNCTION

THESE CRIMES OF PASSIONS,

ARE IN THE SAME MANNNER AS YOUR LIPS,

ACCOMPLISHED.

I PAUSE TO REFLECT,

IN RELATION TO THE EXPRESSION CONCERNING THE SUPERIOR QUICKNESS,

IN THE HAND'S ABILITY TO HOODWINK,
. . . . .EVENT THE WINDOWS OF THE SOUL.

FINDING I MUST ANXIOUSLY,
AND WITH MUCH AMICABLE ANTICIPATION,
IMMEDIATELY, AND ALMOST AUTONOMICALY,
ASSURE MYSELF,
. . . . .UPON EXAMINATION,
OF THE STEADFASTNESS,
OF,
MY HEART,
. . . . AND, OTHER PLACES.

Shhh!

By Michael g. Jones

Without my glasses,
I wouldn't even have known,
It was raining,
Out there,
In the square,

If it were not for Dunlop, Firestone, or, N.T.B.,
And that is onlly because of the open window
of opportunity;

A stealth rain,
If ever there was one.

She is a compassionate rain, as well;

With her soothing cool breeze,

To ease;

Healing me from my only moments ago,

Nearly homicidal morbidity,

All over some missing lenses.

Rampant with reminiscent remnants,

Of the rythmic, melodic, runes,

That were the tunes,

Of Smokey Robinson,

I don't even have to wipe these away.

Yes, this Quiet Storm has cruised,

My blues,

Away from here.

Silent Rain,......

Will you marry me?

THE SENSUOUS SIGNIFICANT

By Skywalker (a.k.a. Michael G. Jones

12/26/1996

*[First Verse and Chorus]---------------------------

Here she comes!

Here she comes!

Lookin' just like a dream;

Body pulsin' Venus Vibes,......

The kind that make me want to scream!

Be..fore.....I even can,

Her eyes hit me,.....Full Soul Slam!

Mode: Slow Jam!

Michael G. Jones

Damn!.......

Woman! Can't you see,

I have just,

Got to be!

Your Man!

Got to make you understand.

Bay.......Be, can't you tell!

You're Love's got me un...der your spell.-------------------

Please,......Please,....

Baby, please.

I know you want me,

Down on both knees,

......, Crying to make you my Main Squeeze.

Well,.... Woman, that's okay.

That's what I pray for every-day:

For your Love to come my way,

And, I won't let you get away.

*[Second Chorus]

Here she comes!
Here she comes!
Lookin' just like a dream!
Pumpin' pulsin' Venus Waves,
The kind that make me want scream!

Be....fore......I even can,
Her eyes hit me,......Full Body Slam!
Full Soul,
Mode: Jam Slow.

Damn!....
Woman! Can't you see,
I have just,
Got to be,
Your man!
Got to make you understand.
Bay-be, can't you tell.
Your Love's got me un-der your spell!-------------------

Her Bod......y moves in tight.

I know we're gonna do this right.

There's no,..... where i can run.

I know we're gonna have some fun.

There's no,..... where I can hide.

Her Love just can-not be denied.

Her Love just takes me for a ride,

Through a LuciousLoveLandScape,

I nev,.....er want to escape.

*[Chorus 1]

The World can't change my point of view.

The Love I have for you is True.

I hope you feel the way I do.

I hope we stay together, too.

You feel for me, Babe! Me for you!

You for me and me for you!

*[Chorus 2]

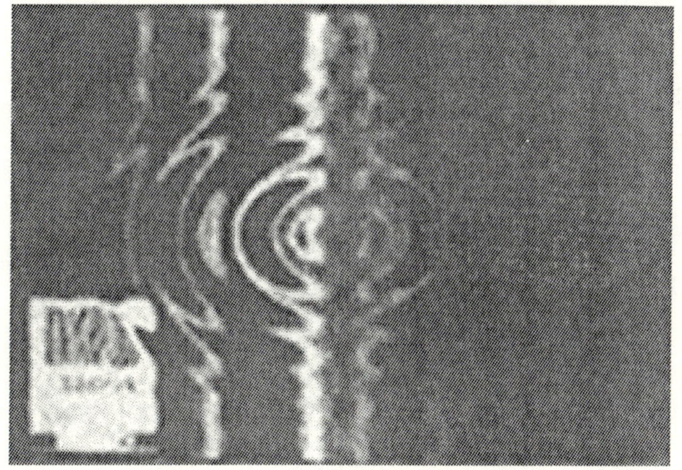

The Death

Of

The Blues

10/18/9 D.1

by

Michael

G.

JONES

e f a t a

s z e v

u a r i

s r n o

e a u

t l r

h

Drifting,

Through this passing,

Transitory,

Nothing.....else quite measures

up!...

To the Majesty

Of the Lady

Story

Briefly, you begin to comprehend,
As, illumination's passing through,
Allows you H.E.A.R.T. to finally mend.

You yearn to contain her GLORY;......

A TREASURE
TO BEHOLD FOR ALL TIME
BUT, HER TIMELESS, PRICELESS BEAUTY, SO
GRACIOUSLY AND GRACEFULLY AVOIDS
THE CAPTURE BY VERSE AND
RHYME

AS HER Heavan sent
Embodiment
Eludes my every line,
While Her Earnest Loving H.E.A.R.T. Exudes A
Preciousness-------------I Must TRust.

She's got the moves,

I've got the notion,

But, her perfection in motion,

Leaves me with only merely this somewhat lyrical commotion,-----

A somewhat inadequate testimony,

To the total devotion,

Of my every Emotion.

Then, She changes her mind;

It's not been hard to find,

That in deed, as well as,

Word

that I have been somewhat kind,

And, that to see her any better,

One would have to be somewhat

BLIND!!!

THE Armored Car Job

By Michael G. Jones

Armored cars,
Armored cars,
Armored cars stay on my mind.
Stacks of cash,
Don't give me a rash,
But I think I'm going blind! [chorus] *

Pulled up to the bumper of a Nice new Armored Car;
My friend, Jesus, by my side.
I sat there feelin' lucid,
And, I dared not look inside,
But, I remember thinkin',
"This babe's a beauty! I'd like to take her for a ride!"

[Chorus]

Guards came stollin' over, out from the
Cambridge
Trust,
Haulin' sacks o' MONEY, just lookin for a robber
to
Dust.
One spotted me there on the rear bumper, so he
gave
His gun a draw.

Me standin' between him and all the Aux Bon Pain
Patrons,
Could have been the last thing we all ever saw.
He was acting like it was his own MONEY!
Or, maybe even Clint's.
The whole thing strikes me, now, as Funny;
As funny as the U.S. Mints.

[Chorus]

When I see an Armored Car, You know, my heart just

Fills with joy.

Taking apart an Armored Car makes me happy, just

Like a child with a brand new toy.

I'd like to pop one open, right now, like some would a

Can of beer.

My trigger finger is itchin', Bad,

Because I think I feel one near.

[Chorus]

"Love Is Driving Me To The Arms Of Another"

by Michael G. Jones

4/97

Driving me to the arms of another.
Love is driving me to the arms of another;
Into the arms of my Precious Lord and Saviour,
Whose Gracious Love is like no other.

Confused and lost, Evil began to surround me.
Hungry for Love is where Darkness found me.
Searching for Love is the Night,
Is when I saw the Light,
Now, I live to Praise and Glorify thee.

Sending me into the arms of another,
Into the arms of my Beloved Lord and Saviour,
Whose Precious Love is Great and like no other.

They said he died for my sin.
It made me shudder.
I tell you he is raised again,
My Sister and Brother;
Born unto eternal Life,
Now, there there's no stress and strife.

Through him the Kingdom of Heaven we will discover.

Driving me to the arms of another,
Love is driving me to the arms of another;
Into the Loving arms of my Personal Friend, and Saviour;
My Blessed Lord and Saviour,
Whose Love is Great and like no other.

Jesus Lives!!!!

Love be still gives and gives, and gives.

He's the Truth, the Light, and the Way.

Praise the Lord!

Jesus Lives, Today!!!!

Jones '97

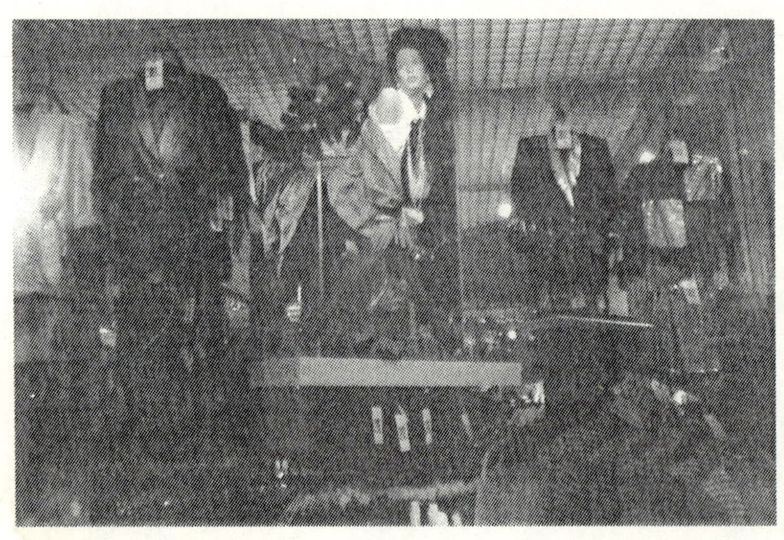

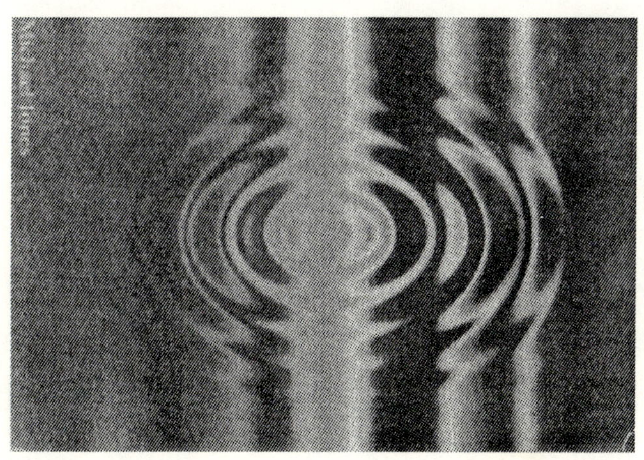

I guess that the best place to start would have been the "Here and Now". This after all, is the "Unfolding". Herein dwells the Primary perrogative and their Analogus Axioms. However, this was not to become the immediate reality. The confusion that was estimated to be, 'the week that followed', was perhaps the result of Flux Fuzz within the fuzz logic modes of the Great Central Cosmic Processing Unix. These are rare, yet as of late, apparently unavoidable. They are Primary amongst the Principal Principles to the principal postulating of primary Primary Principle Postulates pertinent to the postulating of

THE VISITOR CRASHES 1

principles primary to creating creative Creative and Procreative Principal Postulates of Perfection, primarily.

Here or there, on a relatively Insignificant Blue-Green water abundant Biosphere which was, contrary to Poputer Berief, making her way from the outer edge, towards the humanly invisible, but, otherwise oftimes, brilliant center of a Great, (what many of you so arrogantly claim as Your) Spiral Galaxy; the first eleven Elemantal Emmisaries of the Prime had gathered together to create the first Uprighteous Man and Wombman. From neither did they take a rib or rib. From the man they removed the H.E.A.R.T., Hereditary Emotional Apparatus Radiating Tao, or the Way. He was moved and motivated by the Primes oppposite, the Groove, which caused him to grow and flow, but some felt somewhat abberatively though, as what!s being recounted will ultimately show. Wherin, he was adopted by the Great Trine of Force who blessed him with correct cause and course. Finally he returned to the great wisdom and mercy of the Prime, who bestowed upon him true reason and rhyme.

Printed in the United States
5628